Big Sir B and the Monster Maid

Tony Mitton
Illustrated by Arthur Robins

CRAZY CAMELOT

MEET THE KNIGHTS OF THE ROUND TABLE:

King Arthur
with his sword so bright,

Sir Percival,
a wily knight.

Sir Kay,
a chap whose hopes are high,

Sir Lancelot,
makes ladies sigh.

Sir Gawain,
feeling rather green,

Sir Galahad,
so young and keen.

Sir Ack,
who's fond of eating lots,

Sir Mordred,
hatching horrid plots.

Morgana,
Arthur's wicked
sister,

Merlin.
That's me,
your wizard mister!

To the noble Parkers, Sir Oliver, Sir Elliot,
Lady Catherine & Sir Julian.
And to Lady Ann Frost.
From Scribe Tony Mitton

To Sir Hayden Thomas Skerry,
from Arthur Robins

ORCHARD BOOKS
96 Leonard Street, London EC2A 4XD
Orchard Books Australia
32/45-51 Huntley Street, Alexandria, NSW 2015
First published in Great Britain in 2004
First paperback edition 2005

A CIP catalogue record for this book is available
from the British Library.
ISBN 1 84121 498 1 (hardback)
ISBN 1 84362 003 0 (paperback)
1 3 5 7 9 10 8 6 4 2 (hardback)
1 3 5 7 9 10 8 6 4 2 (paperback)
Printed in Great Britain

Back in the Middle Ages,
when knights were just invented,
they sometimes lost their balance
and got their armour dented.

Along with busy combat,
there was lots of dizzy feeling.
Much more than a clout from
a hefty lout,
a crush could send you reeling.

At crazy castle Camelot
some maidens looked so great
that frantic knights got into fights
competing for a date.

I am the wizard Merlin.
I know love can seem icky.
The fizzy wine of valentine
can taste too sweet and sticky.

But here's a tale of pairing up
that really can't be missed.
It's not your usual romance.
It has a gruesome twist.

So let me work some magic.
Get ready...Hocus Pocus!
I'll raise my cup to call it up
and bring it into focus...

The story starts at Camelot.
A feast was about to begin,
when all of a sudden a lady
came weakly stumbling in.

"Is this King Arthur's court?" she wailed.

I hope it's really true
that in this place the knights are ace
and keen on helping you.

"My husband has been kidnapped
by a vast and ghastly knight,
who looks too gross and grisly
for normal guys to fight.

"He tied my husband to his horse
and rode off through the wood.
He said to raise a ransom
or he'd lock him up for good.

"Perhaps there's no one up to it...
Is it too much to ask?
There may be no knight equal
to such a scary task?"

“Not equal to it!?” Arthur cried,
and jumped up from his throne.

I'll set off in the morning
and do the job alone!

“But sire,” said good Sir Gawain,
“to fight a giant needs two.
Besides I'm getting bored round here.
I need a job to do.”

So, as the sun was rising,
the three of them set out.
The lady led them off to meet
this fearful, lumbering lout.

She led them far across the plains
to the Forest of Inglewood,
where a spooky lake lay glistening
and an awesome castle stood.

The castle rose from an island
of dark and rugged rock.
And as it loomed above them,
their knees began to knock.

All of a sudden the drawbridge
came down with a monstrous *thwack!*
Then a massive guy with a gleam
    in his eye
stomped out and boomed,

This knight stood huge and hefty.
His sword shone large and mean.
His armour must have weighed a ton.
His boots were size sixteen.

Brave Arthur gulped and swallowed.
He meant to stand his ground.
But when he tried to challenge the thug
his lips let out no sound!

He couldn't draw his trusty sword.
His arm seemed stuck to his side.
He couldn't even scratch his nose
however hard he tried.

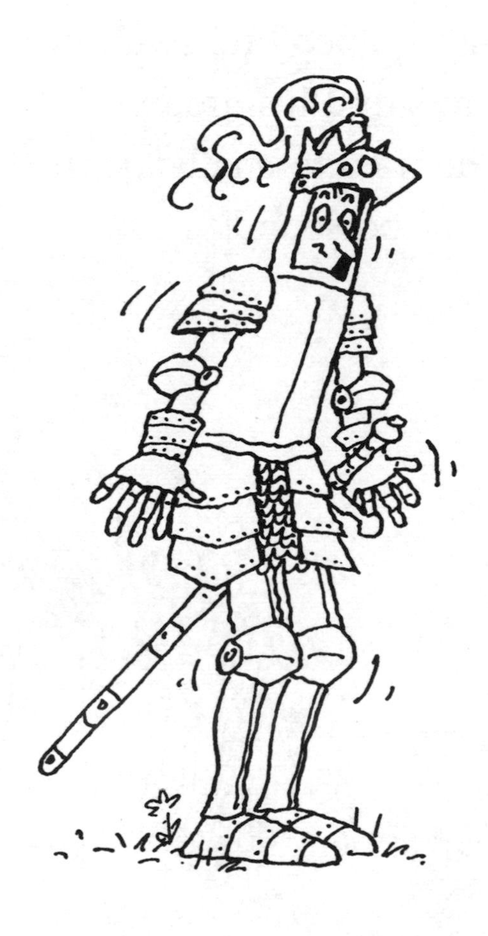

“Tee-hee!” cried out the lady.

It's working really well.
Morgana La Fay, my mistress,
has cast a sticky spell.

(La Fay was Arthur's sister,
and jealous of his crown.
She was up to her witchy tricks again
to bring her brother down.)

"You noble knights," the lady teased,
"are brave, but, oh, so dim.
This chap you see is Big Sir B.
I'll leave you both to him."

So Arthur simply stood there.
All he could do was wait.
A snuffing out by this great lout
would seem to be his fate.

But, “Grrrrrrrr,” the hulking
giant growled,
“to break out from this spell,
there’s just one way to do it, right?
So listen as I tell.”

If you can bring the answer
to the question that I ask,
then you’ll go free from bad old me –
you’ve one year for the task.

"So here's your tricky question.
I ask you only this:
What thing is it that women think
will bring them real bliss?

"Now, don't go blurting answers.
You'll get it wrong, I fear.
Just ask about and check it out
and tell me in a year.

"And if you bring the answer,
then both of you go free.
But if you get it wrong, you'll face
a grisly death from me!"

With that, the villain vanished.
The naughty lady too.
So Arthur and Gawain set off
to do what they must do.

They rode the land and asked away
at houses, farms and huts.
Yet all the answers that they got
were full of 'if's and 'but's.

Some women stood and rambled on
and some burst into tears.
And some just grabbed the startled knights
and whacked them round the ears.

They sought an answer plain and clear
without a trace of doubt.
But with the ending of the year,
their time was running out.

With sinking hearts they made their way
back to a certain doom.
Their heads were full of muddled thoughts.
Their guts were full of gloom.

Then down the road came riding
a lady dressed in white.
"Let's ask once more," said Arthur.

But as Gawain called out to her,
"We beg you, lady fair—"
she turned her head to answer him
and gave both knights a scare.

For though she looked so ladylike
upon her shining horse,
her face was like a monster's,
all slobbery and coarse.

She had a wart upon her nose,
a great big gappy grin.
And weird and wiggly whiskers
grew sprouting from her chin.

Remembering their manners though,
as knights so nicely taught,
they gulped and asked her if she knew
the answer that they sought.

"Why yes," replied the Monster Maid,

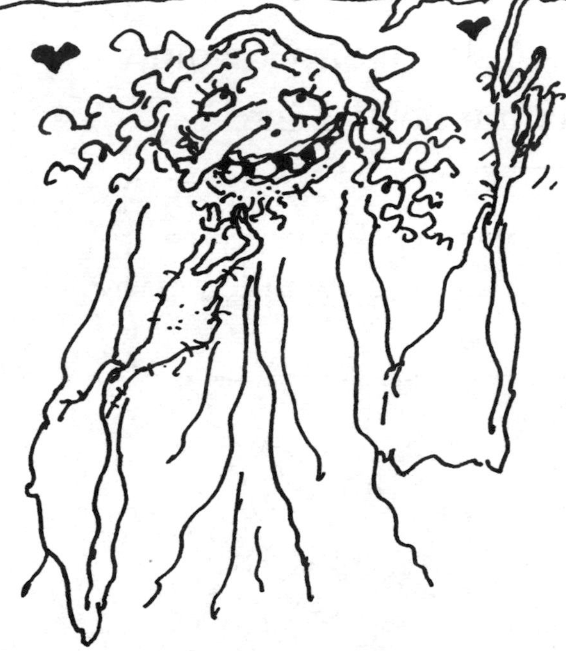

I really think I do.
But in exchange I'd like a husband,
honest, good and true.

"A handsome knight from Camelot
would be the thing for me."
"I don't think," gasped King Arthur,
"we have one going free..."

He felt he couldn't ask a knight
to wed a beast so gross.
And yet, without her answer,
their death was creeping close.

"I'll do it," sighed Sir Gawain,
"for you, my noble King."

To help you stay alive and rule
must be the foremost thing.

The lady leaned to Arthur
and whispered in his ear.
Gawain tried hard to listen,
but, *darn!*, he couldn't hear.

Then off they went together
to meet the giant thug.
And when he saw the Monster Maid,
well, even he said,

But when King Arthur beckoned him
and whispered in his ear,
the ugly thug grinned broadly
and gave a thunderous cheer.

You've done it, smart King Arthur!
You've cracked your sister's spell.
So off you trot to Camelot,
and I can come as well!

The giant had started shrinking
and now he looked alright.
"Well, blow me down!" said Sir Gawain.
"It's Bill, our long-lost knight!"

Then back they rode to Camelot,
each grateful for his life.
But poor Gawain began to dread
his frightful monster wife.

"A deal's a deal," he murmured.

And I'm a famous knight.
There's no way out of this, I guess.
I'll have to do what's right.

The wedding day came quickly round.
The crowds turned up to cheer.
But when they saw the monster bride
they gulped and gawped in fear.

They'd meant to throw confetti
and smile, and shout hooray.
Instead they gasped in horror
and had to look away.

He's marrying a monster,
a beast that looks a fright.
He's done this thing to save the King.
Oh, what a noble knight!

Now, when the grisly marriage
at last had taken place,
Sir Gawain had to hold her hand
and look her in the face.

"According to tradition,
I give my wife a kiss."
He shut his eyes to do the deed,
but then he cried, "What's this!?"

For by his side a beauteous bride
stood where the beast had been.
And she was quite the fairest lass
Gawain had ever seen.

"At last," she sighed, "you charming
chap,
your kiss has cracked the spell.
You also saved King Arthur."

So, there you go, dear readers.
No point in rambling on.
This lass has got her looks back.
Morgana's magic's gone.

The couple seem to be in love.
Yes, that looks pretty certain.
But, *hey!* that's lovey-dovey stuff!
Let's hide them with this curtain...

Oh! What about that secret!?
I haven't told you yet
the thing that women mostly want.
You'd like to know, I'll bet.

I wrote it on a parchment
and tucked it on this shelf.
Oh, fizz! I've gone and lost it.
Well, ask around yourself.

Or, any of you girls out there,
you'll find out soon enough.
So send it me by postcard,
and give me all the guff.

But now it's time for me to go,
I'll pull a monstrous face.
And then I'll turn it beautiful...
... and vanish from this place.

hey!

CRAZY CAMELOT CAPERS

Written by Tony Mitton
Illustrated by Arthur Robins

KING ARTHUR AND THE MIGHTY CONTEST

ISBN 1 84121 714 X £3.99

EXCALIBUR THE MAGIC SWORD

ISBN 1 84121 718 2 £3.99

SIR LANCELOT AND THE BLACK KNIGHT

ISBN 1 84121 722 0 £3.99

SIR GAWAIN AND THE GREEN KNIGHT

ISBN 1 84121 726 3 £3.99

SIR GALAHAD AND THE GRAIL

ISBN 1 84362 001 4 £3.99

MORGANA THE SPOOKY SORCERESS

ISBN 1 84362 002 2 £3.99

BIG SIR B AND THE MONSTER MAID

ISBN 1 84362 003 0 £3.99

MEAN MORDRED AND THE FINAL BATTLE

ISBN 1 84362 004 9 £3.99

Crazy Camelot Capers are available from all good bookshops,
or can be ordered direct from the publisher:
Orchard Books, PO BOX 29, Douglas IM99 1BQ
Credit card orders please telephone 01624 836000
or fax 01624 837033
or e-mail: bookshop@enterprise.net for details.

To order please quote title, author and ISBN
and your full name and address.
Cheques and postal orders should be
made payable to 'Bookpost plc'.
Postage and packing is FREE within the UK
(overseas customers should add £1.00 per book).

Prices and availability are subject to change.